SIX CATS
FIND A HOME

SIX
CATS
FIND A
HOME

RICHARD FREEMAN

Matador
Unit E2 Airfield Business Park,
Harrison Road, Market Harborough,
Leicestershire. LE16 7UL
Tel: 0116 2792299
Email: books@troubador.co.uk
Web: www.troubador.co.uk/matador
Twitter: @matadorbooks

ISBN 978 1803130 934

British Library Cataloguing in Publication Data.
A catalogue record for this book is available from the British Library.

Typeset in 14pt Baskerville by Troubador Publishing Ltd, Leicester, UK

Matador is an imprint of Troubador Publishing Ltd

To Robyn for all her helpful advice

SIX CATS FIND A HOME

It was late one afternoon when the six cats finally decided to escape. It wasn't that they were being ill-treated. The humans who looked after them fed them every day, stroked them sometimes and let them run round the room. But these six cats, who were in cages at the far end of the room, had seen other cats being taken away one by one by other humans who came to visit. Yes, these cats would likely be looked after. But the six remaining cats had become friends and they wanted to stay together.

Suzy, the oldest cat, thought out the plan of escape. When it came time to go back in their cages, Twiggy, the black-and-white cat, waited till the humans weren't looking then she loosened the catch on Jinny's cage. A while afterwards, when the humans had gone out of the room, Jinny pushed open the door of her cage and jumped out. Then she leapt high and flicked open the catch on Twiggy's cage. After that, the two cats let out the other four.

"Well done," whispered Suzy.

Ginger, the only male in the group, was freed last. He was a handsome cat. He knew it because the humans kept telling him he was. He had fur that was almost the colour of marmalade. It was Ginger who now led the way. He sprang onto a table and pushed wide a window that had been left open a little. The rest of the cats followed and landed on the grassy ground outside. It was night-time now and the moon was up.

"Now, everyone, run," said Suzy with quiet urgency.

She ran at the front with Jinny. Both cats had completely black fur. Suzy ran smoothly while

Jinny galloped like a horse. Just behind them was Twiggy. Then came Daisy, whose white fur with little red patches showed clearly in the moonlight. Next to her was Minnie, the smallest and youngest of the group. She had black fur, and a tail as thin as a rat's. Ginger had moved to the back of the group, ready to guard against any danger.

The cats ran across fields and past houses, where they could see humans inside. Suzy was looking for an empty house they could get into. Eventually she found one that was promising, quite a large house that was in darkness except for one light. At the side door there was a cat flap. However, the scent of cat was faint, and there was no distinctive smell of humans.

"Ginger and I are going inside to investigate," said Suzy softly. "The rest of you wait by the door."

The two of them then disappeared through the cat flap. It was not long before they returned.

"The house is empty," announced Suzy. "It's safe for now."

The rest followed her through the cat flap and into the kitchen. There was a light shining from the house next door, and the cats, who had very good eyesight anyway, could see round the room clearly.

"I'm hungry," cried Daisy.

Ginger went to the fridge.

"Let's see what's in here," he said and quickly pulled open the door with a single paw.

"Look, food," said Jinny. "Lots of it."

She jumped onto a shelf and pushed out packets of what seemed like food. Soon the cats were ripping them open with their sharp claws and were eating salmon and chicken. The packet of bacon had teeth marks on it but no one had been able to open it, not even Ginger.

Minnie decided she would see what was in the fridge herself. She climbed up onto the shelf and walked over a packet of eggs. Two of the eggs cracked open and right away Minnie's legs were covered in goo. She jumped back onto the floor and began cleaning herself frantically with her tongue.

"Oh, Minnie," said Suzy. "You're all gooey."

She and Twiggy helped to clear the sticky mess from Minnie's legs and tail. Then Jinny started to groan.

"My tummy hurts," she complained.

"No wonder," said Suzy. "You're eating cheese."

"I'm hungry," replied Jinny. "I like cheese."

Suzy looked round the room. "Where's Daisy?"

"Here I am," came Daisy's voice.

The others looked up and saw her sitting on a blanket in the airing cupboard.

"She's found somewhere warm," said Twiggy.

"She always does," remarked Ginger.

Suzy spotted a cupboard above the fridge.

"I wonder if there's any more food in there," she said.

"I'll look," offered Twiggy.

She jumped up onto the fridge and made another leap at the cupboard but only managed to land on top of it. She got down and tried again with the same result.

"It's no good," she said. "I keep going right over it."

Jinny, who declared she was feeling better, volunteered to have a try. When she sprang from the fridge she flicked the doorknob with a paw and the cupboard slowly opened. She landed back on the fridge at the far end.

"There you are," she said simply.

"You're good at that, aren't you Jinny," Suzy observed.

"Look, there's some biscuits," exclaimed Twiggy. "I bet they're for the cat that lives here."

"She won't mind if we have some," said Ginger.

Twiggy, who hadn't succeeded in opening the cupboard, wanted to be helpful by fetching the biscuits. She leapt up and pushed the packet off the shelf. The top of the packet was open and the biscuits scattered all over the carpet, with a few landing on the fridge. The cats were on the biscuits in an instant and ate them almost as quickly as a vacuum cleaner could suck them up. At last there were only a few crumbs left, but the cats had eaten enough for now. Ginger went to the front room and came straight back.

"Let's go in the other room," he suggested. "It's warmer."

"Come on, Daisy," Twiggy called out.

Ginger pushed the fridge door shut. He didn't know why he needed to do it any more than he knew how he could open it. He was only sure there was food inside. He reflected he must have learned it somewhere.

The door to the front room was open just wide enough for the cats to get inside.

"Yes, it's warm here too," said Daisy.

The cats climbed onto the sofa or on chairs and stretched out. Minnie lay on a cushion and very soon fell asleep, lying on her back with her paws in the air.

"I'll stay awake for a while," said Ginger. "Just in case any creature gets in."

"Wake me if they do," Suzy told him.

"Who'd get in?" asked Twiggy, who was a little drowsy.

"They'd have to be quite small," said Ginger. "I almost had to squeeze through the flap. We'd be able to see them off."

Twiggy seemed happy with this answer and started to close her eyes. Later, when the cats began to wake up, they saw by the murky light coming through the open curtains that it was almost morning.

Suzy yawned. "We're going to need some more food. We'll have to go outside to find it."

"We should do it before it gets too light," suggested Ginger.

The cats moved slowly through the house and out the cat flap. Ginger warned the others not to make any noise for there were humans living in the house next door.

"If anyone needs to do their business," put in Suzy, "do it out here in the garden."

There was a refuse bin at the side of the garage, and it was so full of plastic bags that the lid had not been closed properly. Every cat could sense there was food in the bags. Ginger and Suzy took turns jumping up to tear open a bag. Then they threw or pushed onto the ground as much of the contents as they could manage. After that they joined the others below and started to eat up all the bits of food they could find, ignoring anything that was rancid or tasteless. It wasn't long before they finished.

"There wasn't that much," said Ginger.

"It'll do for now," replied Suzy.

The two cats saw that the others were sitting in a circle in the yard with their tails wagging furiously. In the middle of the circle was a creature, keeping very still. Suzy recognised it straightaway.

"Don't worry," she explained. "She's only a hedgehog. She's harmless. But keep away from all those needles on her back. They're very sharp."

The cats went very slowly one after another through the cat flap. Jinny stopped and stared at the hedgehog.

"She won't come in," said Suzy. "She'll just eat any scraps of food we've left, then she'll go."

Back in the front room the cats were now feeling frisky. The morning light was shining through the window. Minnie found a table-tennis ball and she started to push it around and chase it. After a while she bumped into Suzy, who trapped the ball with her paw. A moment later the ball squirted away and Minnie went after it, missed it and slid into the wall. She wasn't hurt but her fur was ruffled. Daisy went over to join her and the two of them tried to grab each other's tails. Jinny watched a spider with interest until it disappeared under the sofa. Suzy and Twiggy livened up too and scampered around the room. Ginger jumped up onto the front window sill, curious to see what was outside.

Suddenly he called out, "I can see humans. Hide, everyone."

He flattened himself on the sill and stayed very still. Suzy went into a dark corner of the room and checked that the others had hidden too. She couldn't see Minnie but presumed she was with them.

Two humans came to the window and peered inside. They were a man and a woman, both middle-aged. At that moment Suzy caught sight of Minnie, who was on the mantelpiece moving easily between the ornaments there.

"Minnie, come down," Suzy whispered urgently.

Minnie leapt off the mantelpiece. Unfortunately she brushed against one of the ornaments and it dropped after her. Suzy managed to catch the object on her back with only a little discomfort and it fell on the carpet without making a noise. She hoped that because Minnie's fur was all black the humans hadn't spotted her.

The woman said, "I thought I saw something."

All the cats remained motionless.

"They haven't come back yet, have they?" the woman went on.

"Tomorrow, I think they said," replied the man. "I can't see anything."

"What's that in the window?" said the woman.

"It's a toy cat, I think," said the man. "They're very lifelike, aren't they!"

He paused and then said, "Come on, there's no one there."

The two humans moved away from the window. Suzy waited till she could no longer hear their footsteps then she ventured from her hiding place. Slowly the other cats emerged too, with Ginger coming down from the window sill.

"That was close," he said.

The cats all rested for a while. At last Suzy raised her head and spoke.

"I know it's not dark yet but we'll be hungry soon. It means going outside again."

"We could go out two at a time," suggested Twiggy. "The humans might not see us."

"It might work," said Suzy, "but it's best if we all go together. Get it over quickly."

"We'll be all right if we stay close to the trees," said Ginger.

Shortly the cats went out the flap, this time into the garden. Birds could be heard twittering in the trees but Suzy knew they were small and posed no danger. There was a little pool of water by the bushes and, since the cats were all very thirsty by now, they spent a minute or two lapping the water up. Twiggy suggested she climb a tree so she could see if there were any more refuse bins they could raid. Suzy thought this was a good idea.

Then Ginger said, "I'll look in the next few gardens to see if it's safe."

Just after Ginger left, Daisy suddenly cried out, "What's that?"

In a small patch of soil was a creature, long and thin, which in the shade of the bushes looked dark grey. It was wriggling violently and Daisy kept putting out her paw as though she wanted to touch it.

"It's just a worm," said Suzy. "It's harmless."

"It looks a bit squishy," observed Daisy. "I wouldn't want to eat it."

"We might have to if we don't find anything else," declared Jinny.

Ginger returned and said, "Where's Minnie?"

"I can't see her," said Suzy anxiously.

"There she is," cried Jinny. "In the long grass."

Minnie was jumping up and down, sometimes disappearing from view. The others, apart from Twiggy, who was still up in the tree, went to see what was going on.

It wasn't just Minnie jumping up and down. There was a mouse doing it too. Minnie stopped and looked at her friends. The mouse made its escape into the bushes.

"Shall I get it?" asked Daisy.

"No, it wouldn't make much of a meal," remarked Suzy. "Unless there's a lot of them."

Twiggy had come down from the tree and joined the others.

"I can see something that might be food not far away," she told them.

She turned to go and the others followed, keeping in the undergrowth as much as possible. When they reached a particular garden they stopped. After a few moments they crept forward until they were close to a refuse bin that was over full like the one they'd found before.

"We need to keep very quiet," said Ginger in a low tone.

He was the first to jump on the refuse bin, and he tore open a plastic bag with his claws, as before. Then Suzy did the same, with Twiggy and Jinny right behind. Daisy jumped up too, and made it onto the bin at the second attempt. Minnie didn't want to be left out and to everyone else's surprise she managed to land on top of the bin at the first go, though she had to scrabble a bit so she didn't fall off.

The cats stayed perched on top of the bin, chewing scraps of food contently. All of a sudden they heard a door opening and they instantly sprang off the small mountain of bags and darted to the cover of some bushes, where they kept very still, their hearts beating fast.

The humans, another man and woman, had come out into the yard. The cats couldn't see them clearly through the bushes but they could hear what the couple were saying.

"Look at this mess," the woman said. "I hope that fox hasn't come back."

"I'll sweep it up," said the man with a sigh.

The cats sneaked away and then ran as fast as they could back to their garden, where they felt safe.

Everyone had got their breath back and they were about to decide whether to look for another refuse bin when together they caught sight of what looked like a big bushy tail moving through the long grass. Twiggy moved forward a little to see who it belonged to then she said, "Is that a fox?"

Suzy had seen a fox somewhere before and she remembered they weren't usually friendly.

"I think so," she said. "We'd better go in the house."

It was Ginger who knew the danger.

A moment later he called out sharply, "He's coming. Everyone run."

There was a wild dash for the cat flap. Ginger was the last one through, then he and Suzy turned round and waited. A few moments passed, then the flap started to open and the fox's head appeared. It seemed that the flap wasn't wide enough for the fox to get through but he kept trying to push himself forward as though he could squeeze in somehow. Suzy and Ginger were taking no chances. They flashed their claws at him again and again, spitting all the time, trying to fight him off. Suddenly the fox backed away and in a moment had disappeared.

"That was close," said Ginger.

Suzy comforted Minnie, who was trembling with fright, and she promised her that the fox couldn't get inside the house. The cats went back to the front room, where they instinctively felt safe. After a time they felt calm and even managed to sleep a little. They woke with a start.

The front door had opened. The cats all found hiding places and waited to see what happened. A human, an oldish woman, came into the room. After tut-tutting a few times, she said to herself, "How did all this cat hair get everywhere."

Then she went out the room, leaving the door only slightly ajar. But she could be heard talking to herself, saying, "All these crumbs. I hope it was just a cat. I hate mice. Oh, I'll clean it up tomorrow."

Once the woman had left the house the cats relaxed and stretched out. Daisy went to the airing cupboard, having to push her way through the narrow gap at the door.

All was peace for a while. Then a faint sound caught Jinny's attention.

"I can heat a scratching noise," she said.

She moved towards the door. "It's coming from over here."

Suzy and Ginger went up to her and listened. The scratching was quite loud.

"Daisy, is that you?" said Suzy.

There was no reply.

"That's not Daisy," said Ginger. "I know that smell. It's a rat."

No one spoke for a few seconds.

Then Twiggy's voice cut the air. "Daisy's out there."

"Keep Minnie back," Suzy called out.

Then she said to Ginger, "Can you open the door a bit with me."

"The rat'll get in," Ginger warned her.

"I want it to," answered Suzy. "Get ready, everyone. Don't let it bite you."

She and Ginger tugged at the door several times and it opened a little. At once the rat slipped through the gap, baring its sharp teeth. Suzy flew at it and Ginger jumped on its back. The shocked rat wriggled free and belted through the kitchen, with Suzy and Ginger right behind, trying to grab its long tail. Jinny and Twiggy followed, and even Minnie joined in the chase. The rat shot out of the cat flap, which swung violently for a few seconds.

"We won't see that rat again," declared Ginger.

Daisy jumped down from the cupboard.

"I thought I heard a noise," she said.

Suzy showed her relief by touching Daisy's forehead with her own.

"You've got a hard head, Daisy," she remarked. "It's all the stroking you get from the humans."

The incident with the rat had shaken the cats, and they retreated to the front room and lay together in a pile, where they very soon went to sleep. When they woke their hunger had returned. It was still light outside but they were ready to risk it. But just as they were about to go they heard the front door open for a second time and they hid again.

A few moments later a woman came into the room. By chance she caught sight of Minnie.

"There's a little cat here," she called out.

A man appeared and said, "How did it get in. Look, there's more here."

The cats crept out of their hiding places and gathered round Minnie.

"My goodness," cried the woman. "There's six of them."

"I must have forgotten to fasten the cat flap," said the man. "I'll put Fluffy upstairs. She wouldn't like seeing any other cats in here, certainly not half-a-dozen of them."

"They're not wild," the woman said. "They look clean and well fed. Maybe they belonged to someone who couldn't afford to keep them."

"They're not wearing collars," noted the man. "I suppose we should call the authorities."

"Jack and Ellen are looking for a cat," said the woman. "Maybe they'll take them."

"Good idea. They should be at home," replied the man. "I'll put Fluffy in the bedroom first. Won't be long. I'll close the door."

The woman inspected the cats, who came forward hesitantly and let her stroke them.

"You're little sweethearts," she cried as the purring got louder.

When she stroked Daisy, she said, "You've got a hard head, haven't you."

She straightened up and remarked, "You all must be thirsty. I'll get you some milk."

When she left the room she made sure the door was shut properly.

"What do we do now?" Twiggy asked Suzy.

"We'll have to stay here and see what happens," Suzy answered.

Right now the cats were happy to have the milk the woman brought in. They had just about lapped it all up when the man came back. He ushered in two more humans, a man and a woman, who were quite young. He told them he was going to make a few phone calls then he went out the room again. The woman who lived in the house asked the visitors if they wanted some tea and left them with the cats.

"Look at them all," cried the young woman.

The young man patted Ginger on the head. Then the young woman spotted Minnie and picked her up.

"She's so cute," she said. "She's hardly more than a baby."

The young man laughed. "You mean a kitten."

"Ah, now she's putting her claws in my neck," the young woman said.

"Shall I take her from you?" the young man asked her.

"It's all right," responded the young woman, "it doesn't hurt. She's purring. Now she's nipping my cheek. She's just being affectionate."

She gently put Minnie down on the floor and regarded the other cats.

"They look so sad," she observed. "Can't we keep them all?"

"What, all of them?" exclaimed the young man.

"We can afford it," the young woman said. "Look, the ginger one is nodding."

"Cats don't nod," said the young man, shaking his head and smiling.

"We've got a nice big garden," said the young woman eagerly.

"I suppose we could put up a fence to keep them from wandering. Chicken wire or something," the young man suggested.

"That's settled then," said the young woman.

"You know if they belong to someone we'll have to give them back," the young man said softly.

"I know but we can look after them for now, can't we?" cried the young woman.

"I just don't want you to get too fond of them in case we can't keep them," the young man said.

Suzy remembered much of what happened afterwards. She and the other cats were ferried in baskets two at a time to the house where the young couple lived, which wasn't very far. There they were made a fuss of and allowed to sleep where they wanted.

Suzy hoped they could stay. But she wondered whether that would happen when next day two women came to visit. She recognised them as two of the humans who'd looked after her and the other cats when they were in cages, and she was worried they would all be taken back there. But the two women only wanted to examine them.

However, next morning a man came and took Minnie away in a basket. The other cats feared they'd never see her again, but she was brought back in the afternoon. They all smothered her with licks until her fur stood up as though she'd been out in a high wind.

The following day the young couple let the cats out into the garden. No fence had been built. The young couple kept an eye on them and made sure they didn't leave the garden. Eventually though, they were able to roam further, sometimes on their own or in small groups. On occasions they visited the house they had first stayed in, where they had raided the fridge and encountered the fox and the rat. The man and woman were happy to see them. The cat Fluffy was prepared to sniff noses with any of them but no more. She seemed to be telling them this was her territory. They could pass through the garden but that was all.

But the six cats didn't mind. They were content in their new home. They'd been able to stay together after all.

Lightning Source UK Ltd.
Milton Keynes UK
UKHW020858150322
400081UK00007B/301